Mr Rowan
The Woodcutter's Story

Written and Illustrated by Mark Walker

FOREWORD

'Mr Rowan. The Woodcutter's Story' is loosely based on my life's experience of doing show gardens throughout the country.

I was prompted to write the story after years of giving talks within the Southwest promoting our organisation, Walker's Garden Retreats. I was driven by an overwhelming and previously unacknowledged passion and enthusiasm to contribute something towards local charities, but what I didn't realise until much later was that sometimes, acting upon a deeply held personal conviction to the exclusion of all else can unwittingly result in alienating those closest to you, and indeed, adversely affect your own business and financial concerns.

Fortunately I have been supported throughout by my partner, Jayne, and it is she and many of the people I have met and talked with over the years who form the inspiration behind the writing of this story.

Jayne, this story is dedicated to you.

Thank you for standing by me.

Part One

Chapter 1

Mr Rowan

To achieve their goals in life there are those who believe in fate and those who believe in good luck but for Angus Rowan, his driving force was always honest hard labour and a healthy, honest lifestyle. He was a straightforward man who led a simple life with his devoted wife Poppy, but he harboured a dream that there was something more for him than just the normal day to day grind. His job was that of a woodcutter from which he earned his living, selling wood and charcoal at the village market and he also tended a few gardens to help ends meet. One of his clients was Rory Birch who owned the very exclusive hop fields. Another was Okely Oak who made his fortune selling trinkets of gold and silver to the rich. Both of these clients were fine upstanding people in their community. Angus appreciated their status but seldom asked himself why he wasn't in their league until one day someone suggested that he should enter the local village garden competition.

Angus had always been admired for his gardening skills and his vegetables were the envy of the village, but even so, it took all Rory Birch's skills to persuade Angus to enter the competition, telling him that it would be a bit of fun, and arguing that after all. 'What possible harm could come of something so trivial as a local event?'

Angus had always tended his vegetable plot with pride. Sustainability was at the heart of his philosophy and he proved this year by year when the seeds he had sowed earlier in the year re-emerged on the table as the finest food in the hamlet as they were served by Poppy. As a team they had never asked for anything more, but the local vegetable competition was to alter this balance.

ANGUS & POPPY ROWAN

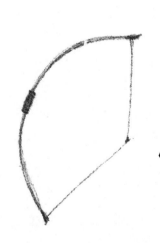

ROWAN
Sorbus aucuparia
AKA: Angus and Poppy

This tree namesake also, known as mountain ash, gives colour and berry all year round, very dependable, and requiring little fuss. Connected to ancient witchcraft, it has a norse name of runa, meaning 'a charm'. The berry is made into jelly which is eaten with game and rich in vitamin C. It was once used for long bows instead of Yew, plus widely used for making tool handles. A graceful tree which grows up to 65ft (20m) high.

Chapter 2

Trendlewood Vegetable Show

Angus had always taken the local Trendlewood Vegetable Show with a pinch of salt. He knew his vegetables were the cream of the crop but he was never one to boast about them. The village show attracted everyone who knew anything about gardening, people like: Dicky Elder who was famous for his sweetcorn, a rough looking chap with a good head of hair; or Rosie Hip whose prize winning runners always put her way up front, a fair maiden with a very prickly disposition; but the man who stood out above them all was Harry Hawthorn whose marrows were the largest in the patch and who had won the Wooden Spade 5 times in a row. Harry was a man of strong stature who refused to bow down to anyone. Angus of course, knew of him and was at ease enough to enjoy good natured banter with him as well so many of the other locals.

The problem was that Angus seemed blissfully naïve about any problems that might come about from his entry into the competitive world of Village Shows. Poppy on the other hand was very mindful and soon began to detect the very slight changes in his behaviour.

Chapter 3
Poppy Rowan

Poppy Rowan was a dutiful wife who carried out her chores with no fuss and without complaint; she was contented with herself and with her life. She was still a bonny woman who would never let her husband down. The love between them was strong and deep, never publically displayed, with both of them happy to keep their private lives to themselves.

Sadly she was unable to bear children but she never brooded over this fact, content in the knowledge that this was what fate had dealt her and it was not for her to question it. She loved walking in the woods early in the morning, returning each day with wild flowers for the breakfast table. The woods always obliged her and never let her down in any season. It was as though her warmth was lapped up by the trees and that they enjoyed her company. Her songs would brighten up a dull day when the birds failed to sing.

As she saw it supporting her husband in this show was a moment of personal pride, and, she mused, 'What harm can come from a bit of fun for a change?'

Chapter 4

The day of the Show

Finally the day of the show arrived. This year had yielded a bumper crop of vegetables and there was huge expectation that the prize vegetables would be spectacular. Prize blooms were on display from many villagers; Honey Suckle, a quiet, shy, scented woman who had climbed her way slowly through the ranks, had her usual display of woodland orchids; proud housewives displayed a delicious array of cakes including Granny Bonnet with her usual entry of Fruit of the Loom fruitcake. The Village Hall had been booked several months ago to accommodate this harvest feast and the arrival of the whole village looking for a taste of whatever might be on offer.

The judges were the local priests and conjurers who liked to make their presence felt by parading in all their finery. One by one the contestants would appear, presenting their offerings like a ceremonial blessing to the gods. Most were light hearted, just enjoying the occasion, some were more optimistic of a prize rosette, and then there were those who were almost smug about their anticipated success, you know the sort, the ones who were almost contemptuous about everyone else, seeing them only as making up the numbers. Harry Hawthorne was such a person, who at this point did not fully realise that there was one person who might just knock him off his pedestal, and that person was Angus Rowan.

Chapter 5

The Judging

All but one entrant had arrived. The villagers had begun to think that Angus would not show. Some were quietly hoping that he would not arrive, but others were disappointed that he was late. The judges were impatient to begin, they were getting hungry but the cake tasting was the last in the categories and so they began their judging of the vegetables. In true judicial fashion any vegetable that according to them did not come up to standard would get the chop – literally, chopped with a sword. The display tables became a site of such ruin that was terrible to see. And then, just in the nick of time, Angus appeared pushing a bodged together wheel barrow full of the biggest and most perfect vegetables imaginable. There was a gasp from the audience as he announced his attention of entering all categories and proceeded to lay out his vegetables on the table supplied. The judges were amazed and in awe of his eclectic array of mixed vegetables. The decision was unanimous. Heads dropped in disbelief as Harry Hawthorn's marrow got the ceremonial chop and Angus was crowned overall winner and rightfully awarded the coveted Wooden Spade.

To the admiration of his wife, watching from back in the wings, Angus stood proudly holding his prize and being congratulated by all; some people who he knew and admired, some that he just recognised from the village. It seemed like they were all his friends, at least until the mead ran out and they began drifting away. Angus

RORY BIRCH

Broadly admired throughout the hamlet, he stands on a par with Okely Oak but stands alone on his strength of character. This sacred tree, revered by the pagan Celtics as possessing powers of renewal and purification. It's twigs were used to drive out spirits from an old year. Aptly then, it's twigs were converted into besom brooms, plus it's wood used for tool handles. Hieght 50ft (15m)

SILVER BIRCH
Betula Pendula
AKA: Rory Birch

enjoyed it all and for the first time saw the possibility of a different future. It was indeed the beginning of something new but what he did not know was that this would also lead to his fall.

Chapter 6

After the Show

That night, fresh from his victory, Angus lay awake his mind racing with ideas. He had enjoyed the day; he had liked the admiration and was beginning to think that he wanted more of it. For the first time in his life he had won something and he wanted to win more and more. Poppy saw that Angus was deep in thought and left him to bask in his moment of glory. Inwardly she thought that the spade would come in nice and handy for lifting the turnips.

The following morning Angus awakened still consumed with his recent success. Poppy was quick to notice the slight change in him but she kept her thoughts to herself. Her head was full enough with all the winter tasks ahead, something Angus had always been quick to remind her of, but this time he was distracted and his ideas were clouding his normal duties.

Angus left for work promptly enough after a quick slurp of gruel but he forgot to kiss Poppy as he left. In all of their 20 years together, he had never left like that and Poppy was left on the doorstep in the cold morning air, staring after him and wondering.

As the weeks progressed well into the winter the atmosphere at home was as cold as the weather. Bit by bit Poppy noticed slight changes in Angus. Their routine began to shift subtly; tasks were forgotten and it was as though Angus were in a different space to her making her feel very uncomfortable. Poppy wanted little out of her life, a warm and comfortable home, food for the table and the company of her husband. But now Angus was coming home after a full day's work with only half of his usual wages and with little or

HARRY HAWTHORN

This small tree is testament to Harry's resolve. Hawthorn is commonly laid for hedging, but Harry refuses to be laid or beaten. Hawthorn greets the summer for it's flower 'may'. Pagans believed that removing a hawthorn invites peril.

HAWTHORN
Crataegus monogyna
AKA: Harry Hawthorn

Such is it's strength, in medieval times to bring it indoors was to court disaster. It is famous in Glastonbury for being the 'Holy Thorn', the place where Joseph of Aramathea planted his hawthorn staff in the ground, where it sprouted the Holy tree.
Height 45ft (14m).

nothing in the way of conversation or companionship. In the end she had to ask him why this was happening. His answer was that the work was slowing down, but this was only partially the truth.

Chapter 7

The Tempting of Angus

You see Angus had started to dream and to dawdle through the day; his mind was not set on the day to day tasks only on dreams of more fame and fortune. Then one day he came across a man who would offer such gifts but what Angus did not realise was that the price of this would be his very soul. The man he met was Mr Goldie Maple, a man who far exceeded his name in more ways than one. He was a kind of modern day agent and PR representative for a show called The Fantabulous Floral Fortnight held each year in the Middle Counties. Angus's reputation for growing exceptional vegetables had reached the ears of Goldie and after speaking with several of the villagers Goldie knew that Angus was ready for a fresh challenge. Goldie, as the saying goes could sell daffodils to the Welsh and thistles to the Scots and was possessed of that overwhelming ego that would make the unsuspecting such as Angus feel good.

The Fantabulous Floral Fortnight was an annual event held in the Middle Counties and this adored show was a celebration of harvest and floral achievements. Mr Maple drew all the prizewinning exhibitors from each hamlet enticing them to enter to try to win the Champion of Champion shield. Some would immediately refuse to enter, some would say that they would give some thought to it but in the end a small percentage would enter, namely, those foolish enough or gullible enough to be sucked into Mr Maple's web of charms and dreams. Sadly, this is what happened to Angus; it was like an accident waiting to happen. He was completely ensnared by all the pipe dreams and visions of fame Goldie dangled before him, so how could he refuse?

The Fantabulous Floral Fortnight was a show in two parts. The first week was a festival of music, mead and mayhem. The show would pay homage to the Sun God of all 4 seasons. Priests from all corners of the world would come, exerting their powers and displaying their prowess. The show also drew a mixture of band stars, gangsters and villagers all gathered together in a large field with bootleg mead, fake gold and villains everywhere. The faint hearted were not encouraged to attend but if they chose to come the organisers made it clear that it was at their own risk and that they, the promoters, would take no responsibility if they fell ill or lost money.

Woodwind music was the normal choice of music but many would dance to the sound of the beat of a different drum. Local law enforcement from the shires attended in a loose capacity; all it took was a bribe of some good mead for them to turn a blind eye to most of what they witnessed. They would intervene, if they could stand up, if matters got out of hand around the bar area, but other than that, they did little. The entrance fee was merely a penny but the profits came from the inflated cost of food and mead. Thievery was rife especially from the drunks and the many 'chancers' who were there. If caught they would be forced to relinquish their booty to the local enforcement officers who subsequently would make them sit and watch them consume it all.

All in all the people who attended were good natured and seldom stayed for more than 2 days, thus allowing the next batch of villagers to repeat the same scenarios. This would carry on for a full 7 days until either the ground got soggy or the mead ran out. I am sure you can imagine the sight.

One reveller called Sticky Sap was considering going to a similar event down South, if he could get a horse. This event was being organised by a some druids who had this crazy idea of creating a stone circle with stones that would come all the way from Wales. Some say it will never happen, but who knows?

The second week of the show was all about the floral and vegetable prowess of the finest growers in the known land. Seldom did people who had attended in the first week come again during the second part – they were too busy dealing with their thumping heads. This made room for a more civilised group of people whose skills in horticulture were the envy of their parishes. They were the elite of growers, whose lives were dedicated to one variety of plant, perfecting their blooms or vegetables to the very peak of excellence and then perfectly presented.

People like, Victoria Plum who grew perfect pumpkins, Cox Pippin with his perfect plums and Mr Greaves dared anyone to grow a bigger, more perfect marrow than he. Felicity Foxglove was the finest grower of cyclamen and some talked of her being a judge next year. But this was quickly dashed by Francis Fern who knew that her periwinkles had impressed them more.

Such was the rivalry between them that you could cut the atmosphere with a blunt axe.

One by one the growers would appear; some by foot, others by cart and the 'inbetweeners' who would hitch a ride by some unwitting coachman. A great canopy was suspended over 4 great oaks to house this assorted set of civilians. Each competitor had one small log on which to present their exhibit, some would even bring their own log for better display. These of course were the wealthy ones who did it just because they could.

Once the exhibits were neatly and proudly displayed the judging could begin. The judges were similar to those who judged the exhibition gardens outside; in they would come, full of the sense of their own importance and all marching in step with each other. There were a few low murmurings from the crowd but not loud enough to intrude. These fine fellows were the best in their field and between them they had won many a Golden Turnip in their distinguished careers. They all seemed to have adopted the same dress code of woven woollen wraps on their heads plus twisted tartan tweed jackets and trousers. To look any different would signify a lower class of person and make them indistinguishable

FANTABULOUS FLORAL FORTNIGHT

from the lesser exhibitors in their jute jumpers and sack sarongs. They would keep their distance from ordinary folk until asked by Mr Maple to approach them. Like the judges in the garden category they would judge from the best part of the canopy namely, the part that didn't leak.

The winner of each category would be boldly announced to the waiting exhibitors and excited visitors by an exuberant Mr Maple. There were never any surprises, Francis Fern for her fine periwinkles and Mr Greaves for his magnificent marrow

Congratulations would be offered to both and somewhat begrudgingly each winner would be awarded a fine shield of oak encrusted in elderflower colouring. All the exhibitors would then be ordered to stand by their stalls for the next 7 days, including those whose dreams had been shattered and were overcome with a sense of failure.

The biggest excitement however was the 5 staged gardens full of theatre and floral brilliance. This main feature of the show was orchestrated by Goldie Maple. He would scour the country looking for vulnerable people to entice to enter. Angus would be such a one, lured by Goldie's words and persuaded by dreams of grandeur. Not forced to enter of course, just persuaded by visions of success.

Chapter 8

Angus and Poppy

The first thing Angus had to do was to persuade Poppy of his vision for better things. That evening over pumpkin pie he announced his decision. Not surprisingly Poppy said she would stand by her husband; she wanted him to follow his dreams and of course she would support him fully, how could she not? He was her husband and she loved him. But time would show that she would come to regret this decision and her patience would be severely strained.

As the months passed their home life began to suffer. The show garden and all the ideas surrounding it began to take precedence in Angus's thoughts and actions. The impetus for the garden was taken from the writer Charlie Coppice and his wonderful book, 'The Magical Fairy Tales of Life at Toadstall'. In his mind's eye already Angus could see a mock timber framed building surrounded by an abundant vegetable patch and rich floral beds.

Poppy couldn't help but notice that the more Angus engulfed himself in dreams of this creation the more his behaviour was a cause of concern. He no longer concentrated on his paid work; the wood was beginning to suffer so that the normal sweet breeze in the air seemed to be turning stale. Angus performed his duties to the woodland in a hasty manner, rushing his logging and leaving some trees in a sorry condition, something he would never have done before. As the months progressed his coppicing became more and more ugly and to her dismay she could see that some trees had been unnecessarily felled to create his garden. To ease her own pain at what she could see Poppy tried singing to the trees but it was as if even they knew that bad rot had set in. Poppy felt her loyalties were being divided but for now she held her tongue and remained loyal to the Angus she had known and loved for so long.

As she looked out she could see that where Angus was partially constructing the garden was actually taking up a large percentage of the plot they had always used for their own food production. Yields next year would undoubtedly suffer. When Poppy gently challenged Angus with this problem he vowed to work harder to make up the shortfall but she could see that this new project was just eclipsing all common sense in him and that she would have to be more resourceful with their meagre food and funds. Taking on a secret job behind Angus's back was just one her radical moves.

As time went on Poppy's friends in the village could see the toll this was taking on her health and that she was becoming more and more weary and one by one they raised their concerns to Angus. Angus was a proud man who believed he had always provided well for his wife and he did not take kindly to these neighbourly concerns. It was as though a breach of trust had been broken between Poppy and Angus in the eyes of the public. Poppy gave up her job and returned to her duties at home to the point of becoming a virtual recluse. She served her penance and assured Angus of her unswerving loyalty, a fact that in his own private way Angus eventually respected.

This was the beginning of the growing distance between Angus and the people he had grown up with. He was learning that fame had a high price. Over and again Angus would explain to Poppy that it would all be worth it for if his garden won the coveted crown at the Fantabulous Floral Fortnight all their money problems would disappear. Nevertheless, to appease her he did try to adjust his workload to compensate in part for the shortfall. Poppy appreciated this and comforted herself with the thought that it was only a garden show and it would be all over by next winter.

Since, in order to satisfy Angus's pride, Poppy had given up her much needed extra paid work, she felt that it fell to her to take on some of the more mundane, day-to-day jobs that Angus would normally do but which still were being missed by him. Jobs like collecting the kindling and chopping the wood for heat and cooking purposes at home. She didn't complain, just got on with it but it soon became obvious that it was putting quite a burden on her small frame.

Angus steadily continued building his creation, preparing every frame in such detail so that it could be loaded onto a wagon and transported and then rapidly reassembled at the show. His attention to detail was immaculate, every dowel was lovingly and perfectly shaped and carved to fit each post hole and carefully stored in the lean-to he had created. Not only did he create the frame for the garden but he was also growing the flowers and vegetables. Every day served up a fresh challenge that would test Angus's resolve, be it work commitments, battling with the elements or dealing with strange pests and diseases. Wild garlic from the woods solved many of his problems but if one plant failed he already had others in stock to replace them. All the time the clock was ticking; would he complete this jigsaw of a garden in time? Would his cart take the load? Would Hercules be able to pull it?

Hercules was a strong Shire horse sired from a champion puller of wood. He came to Angus and Poppy as a gift from a landowner who appreciated Angus's hard work in the woodlands. He was a typical Shire horse, big and strong, never fast but capable of going on working long hours without showing any signs of slowing down. Angus treated him well, almost like one of the family. Sometimes he would spoil him with treats of carrots and apples to accompany his daily horse bag of hay. Hercules slept in a make shift, ramshackle barn that was always dry and had fresh straw for his bed. The furniture consisted of the farm tack and machinery and his company in the evening was Percy the owl when he was not out searching for the mice in Angus's field who in turn were seeking a late night snack of carrots and strawberries. Percy kept the mice in check to help Angus's crop and in return received free board and lodging, a perfect partnership. Hercules never minded Percy after all he had been there long before Hercules.

Nevertheless Hercules too had detected a change in his master's behaviour, it was more rushed, less kindly, but Hercules, like Poppy, was hoping that this was just a temporary problem.

Chapter 9

The Floral festival

The day for the start of the build finally dawned. Angus had already loaded the cart with all the parts of the garden, carefully placed on bulging bags of batons and bolster wood. Angus vaguely wondered if Hercules would be able to pull it but reassured himself that his faithful horse had pulled much more in the past. Finally he bade farewell to Poppy with a peck on the cheek and looked sincerely into her eyes. Any soft, caring words that he might have been tempted to use were banished by a loud and impatient grunt from Hercules. Fortunately Poppy knew her husband well and was just happy for him to be setting off on what she hoped would be the final furlong before settling back into what had been their quiet and contented life together.

Angus's journey took him 3 days to join up with other exhibitors who had had either slightly shorter or even longer journeys to reach the show ground. Many of them were weary and just pleased to have arrived while some more fortunate ones were in a much more boisterous mood; Angus was just keen to get on and settle Hercules to rest with large nose bag.

Goldie Maple, looking fatter, more red cheeked and wearing his usual flamboyant clothing, was booming out greetings to all around. Angus found it all a bit unnecessary and smiled to himself when he heard one exhibitor describe him as 'That circus ring master' and another who said 'Chuck him a trout to make him pipe down'. In the main though it was all good natured banter as people settled into sorting out their plots.

Angus wasted no time in constructing the frame for his garden. He needed to be busy to block out thinking about the fact that this was the first time he had been away from home and admitting how much he was missing Poppy. He looked around at his fellow exhibitors and could see the same quiet determination in many of them. The exception was Mr Blackthorn. He had done many shows over the years and had won several prizes, and he paraded around the garden area, looking at the progress of others with an air of snooty arrogance. Angus had encountered Blackthorn before and neither liked him nor loathed him; he just knew that he was not someone he wanted to get involved with.

What most unsettled Angus was that not only did Blackthorn have more of his own money to spend on his garden than most other competitors but it became obvious that in addition he was being sponsored handsomely by the highly successful flower grower business 'Amazing Blooms'. Angus paced up and down in distress; for him this show was all about winning; he had to go home victorious or live the rest of his life in shame; there was no room for coming second. Desperately he reached deeply into his mind to find a solution and realised that lovely though his blooms were, he needed to buy bigger and better ones if he was going succeed. Six months of really hard toil at home had meant that his garden was already paid for. He had come here with only his reserve cash which was to cover all his and Hercules's needs while away from home. Swiftly, and with no thought for the consequences, Angus decided to spend all of this money on buying new blooms.

After a week of intense construction, planting and very careful, loving placing and pruning of plants and blooms, Show Day dawned. The last of the happy drinkers and chancers from the high spirited first week of the show were finally making their way out just as the more serious garden lovers from all 4 shires began to converge on the grounds. By now Angus was totally drained of energy; for a man of his large stature feeding on foraged wild mushrooms and elder roots was not enough to sustain him. He had sacrificed his normal healthy diet of good bread and ham and game to the point where he was now just running on adrenaline fuelling his belief that he could and would win.

His finished garden was beautiful. Angus's realisation of Charlie Coppice's description of Toadstall was perfect in every detail; a gently winding path led the eye to the timber framed main building with its low cropped thatched roof manicured to perfection. The central front door was flanked by delicately perfumed, glorious blooms and slightly to the side; encased in a low hurdle the finest crops could be seen in the abundant vegetable patch. With the exception of one, each of his rival competitors had come up to Angus and genuinely even if with some inevitable reluctance, expressed their admiration for his work and the beauty of his creation. The one person who did not come to speak to Angus was Mr Blackthorn. Instead he stood well back and glared at Angus with a look of sheer contempt on his

MR BLACKTHORN

This thorny prickly hedgerow plant
is unpleasant to work with, like Mr
Blackthorn it protects it's own, but
wards off others, humans and grazing cattle.
Birds nest among the dense, thorny thickets,
eat caterpillars and other insects from
the leaves, and feast on the berries in
autumn. It flowers early in a period
of cold easterly winds, and produces
sour sloes, used in gin. The Wood has
been used for hay rakes and walking sticks.
A thorny shrub which grows up to 13ft (4m) high.

BLACKTHORN
Prunus Spinosa
AKA: Mr Blackthorn

41

face. Angus sighed quietly but had no time to think anything more about it because the judging was about to begin.

In marched the judges; Mr Maple was at the front and could be seen preening himself, pushing out his stomach and pulling back his shoulders as he led in the splendidly dressed local worthies. As usual, and much to the amusement of the crowds gathered in the arena, Goldie's booming voice could be heard loudly above all the noise and chatter. Angus, however, found himself hoping that one day he might be in that parade and even be at the head of it.

The judges proceeded to the centre of the field, heads turning to observe the show gardens but the only signals the competitors could see were small hand gestures. They then moved round the arena again quietly muttering to each other about slight imperfections and even suggestions of idleness on the part of the gardeners but only the odd word could be heard here and there. The exhibitors stood silently to the side of their gardens knowing how hard they had worked and yet in their uncertainty of the protocol at times like this, not knowing whether they could explain or defend themselves. Suddenly Goldie Maple's booming tones rang out instructing all exhibitors to leave the arena so that the judges could begin to come to their decision. In something of a muddle Angus and the others walked off in different directions, uncertain of which way to turn but all anxious to avoid each other at this nerve racking time. Angus walked out to where Hercules was waiting and pretended to check his reigns and strapping but really he was casting glances over to the judges to see if he could decipher their reactions.

It was a long and agonising wait as the judges went back and forth over their deliberations and Angus felt quite drained by the time they were all told to return to the arena. Mr Maple pompously mounted his wooden pulpit and in his booming voice announced...

'Following great deliberation of all the gardens these fine judges of the middle counties have awarded the Rosewood Bowl to ....'

The pause, theatrical and deliberate on the part of Goldie, was breath-taking for the open mouthed crowd and agonising for Angus and the other competitors and then Goldie continued...

'Mr Blackthorn for his Woodland Idyll'

The announcement was met with a gasp and then silence from the crowd except for the piercing, sneering laughter of Mr Blackthorn. Angus's head sunk in total despair and disbelief. His initial thought was to ask 'Why?' but his action was to walk quickly away just noting from the corner of his eye Mr Blackthorn being congratulated by the judges. A sudden downpour of rain quickly stifled both Blackthorn's crowing laugh and sent all the competitors to seek shelter under the floral canopy.

Not even the magnificent blooms could lift Angus's spirits, he who had always appreciated the colours and the smells of beautiful flowers and shrubs; his defeat had left him colour blind, confused and cast down. He had never contemplated failure in his quest for glory, and now, so far from home, he must face it alone. The rain continued throughout the show, prolonging the moment of leaving to face the long journey home and the reactions of his own village to his failure. During this time Angus realised that he must use the time to buck himself up, he couldn't go home looking and acting like a broken man.

As it turned out Angus's return to Trendlewood was very different from his expectations; the prolonged and significant rainfall over the last week had served to flood his village and the devastation caused was such that Angus's return was not even noticed. The villagers' thoughts were totally concentrated on saving their homes, land and animals from complete destruction. The crops in the surrounding fields were a sight of misery and mayhem. Tamsin Ash had lost her whole strawberry crop to the water's wrath; Thomas Elder was distraught after witnessing his tomato crop falling into the swirling River Axe, all his efforts to save them thwarted by the gale force winds. Angus had returned via the high road and could see so much of the destruction but was relieved to see that his own home looked relatively unaffected. There was some land run off creating small canals through his vegetable plot, but nothing more damaging from what he could see.

Poppy could see him approaching and could tell that he had suffered defeat but she was just counting her blessings that he was safely back and could deal with the leaking roof. She was not going to force conversation with him and gave him a warm welcome and ushered him into the comfort of their humble home. Later Hercules was unbridled and gently pulled to his dry barn of clean straw and a fresh nosebag of carrots and apples. During a hearty meal of pumpkin pie and blackberry cake she told him of the distress of their neighbours and then with no discussion of his recent adventures they retired to bed. Poppy just hoped they could now get on with their normal lives.

Chapter 10

The Following Days

It is often said that a peaceful night's sleep can help to calm the mind allowing people to waken the next day and see things in a clearer way, less aware of irritating thoughts and more concentrated on what is really important. So it was for Angus; his despair of the previous few days gave way to a greater optimism and he found himself thinking about the future again. Wisely, he kept these thoughts to himself, but he didn't fool Poppy and she found his silence worrying.

Weeks passed where an unseasonable amount of rain in the autumn gave way to an exceptionally harsh winter. Angus and Poppy helped out two close friends with simple food and straw which was gratefully received in a period of such great hardship. Angus continued to supply the much needed logs to his clients and any surplus small kindling was given to the neediest. No-one actually

MR OAK

He is a fine upstanding man in his community. Dependable, strong and wise, respected by the local druids as the unsung champion of the village.

The English Oak has large branches from a short trunk which form a massive crown rising to 115ft (35m). For centuries the wood has been used to build houses and the frames for ships. The British Navy was built on Oak.

OAK
Quercus Robur
AKA: Oakley Oak

Sciurus vulgaris
Red Squirrel

asked him how he had gone on at the show, probably because his silence on the subject was all the confirmation they needed and they were reluctant to upset him by probing. Eventually the first signs of spring began to emerge and the buds on the trees and the peeping through of the first early spring bulbs signalled the beginning of the rebirth of the land.

Angus however had found the long frozen winter provided him with seemingly endless time to think back and to brood over his sense of failure and humiliation. For the villagers the autumn floods and the bitter winter meant that their main concern was this year's crop yield and that was all they could think of and talk about. But Angus found their silence to him about the show more painful than any cruel words.

Increasingly his thoughts turned to the next garden idea, bigger and grander than his previous one, such was his desire to prove those judges wrong and to restore his reputation. His garden, the 'Garden of Kings' would require more wood, more plants and even more resources to build. Such was the scale of his vision that he realised he would probably need two carts to transport it.

That evening for the first time he told Poppy about his plans. She listened in silence when he told her of his dream project. He planned to involve the villagers by offering to supply free wood to anyone who would help him build his garden or grow his plants on their plots of land from seeds provided by Angus. In addition he proposed a fundraising event to help buy a new horse and cart to deal with his transport needs. Such was his passion and blind obsession with his plan that Poppy knew no words from her would make him slow down and think things through more clearly. For years Angus had been known as the finest woodsman for miles and miles around. The entire village relied on him to tend to the woodland and to provide good seasoned wood and monster vegetables to them. Yes there were some who took advantage of his kind nature and who scrounged wood and food from him but most of the villagers were more than happy to pay their share in return for top quality and a superbly managed woodland.

ANGUS'S FIRST GARDEN

The previous woodsman had been a very different character. Mr Ivy had been a greedy, clingy man who had nearly destroyed the ancient woodland for his own selfish reward. When one wild and stormy night he had been killed by a falling limb from a neglected Great Oak there was no-one there to save him and no one left to mourn his passing. Poppy knew that the villagers had been so pleased to greet her and Angus when they took over the woodland and recognised at once their kindness and Angus's professionalism. Now her heart was filled with dark fears.

Chapter 11

Poppy's Fears are Realised

Over the next weeks Angus's workload became unbearable. Poppy was also feeling the strain; she would see Angus leave before sunrise and return at sunset too exhausted to give her a kind word or a warm hug to keep her going. Her health began to waver but Angus did not even notice. He was looking more and more gaunt as if his obsession was eating him alive. The new garden took precedence over everything else and even the 7th day, normally a day of rest was sacrificed to building the garden. Angus's stubbornness convinced him that all would be well but increasingly Poppy could see that things were going badly wrong. The more he became immersed in his project the less attention he paid to detail and he would simply brush away her concerns about where the money was coming from and where were the vegetables that she had for so long relied upon to make nourishing food? The only thing that mattered to him was the garden.

The villagers had at first appeared to support his project, but then, why would they not, they were getting a valuable resource free from him in return for just a little bit of time and a small patch of land. They could not, however, really share or understand his

Mr Maple

Field Maple
Acer Campestre
AKA: Goldie Maple

A man of great presence within his fellow peers. Like his tree namesake he is a colourful character that sticks out in a crowd. A Field Maple is a round headed tree with a sinuous trunk that grows up to 85ft (26m). In Autumn his leaf turns amber yellow. The wood has been used to make the violins used by supremo Antonio Stradivarius (1644 - 1737).

passion and soon their early promises began to be forgotten. His plea for volunteers to help build the garden was dashed by more than one excuse ranging from bad backs to lack of time to just sheer indifference. Angus discovered bit by bit how so many of them could talk the talk but ultimately just fail to deliver. Most of the villagers saw Angus's promise of free wood as an opportunity to stock up now and deliver later, collect now grow later. No matter what words of caution Poppy offered Angus continued to trust them and went on supplying more and more wood.

Not even the lack of support for the fundraising event opened his eyes. So far only a handful of close friends had signed up to events like the tug-of-war, the archery contest and the champion ditch jumping; not even the prize of a barrel of beer, promised by the local hostelry could persuade the village drunkards and chancers actually to pledge their support, all they were prepared to promise was they would turn up on the day and enter then. Foolishly Angus accepted this saying that any help would be appreciated and reminding them that they were supporting a good cause.

The 'Garden of Kings' demanded and swallowed up constant resources from the wood; just one turret and palisade required a massive quantity, plus two weeks to build. Poppy looked on in total dismay, in her eyes he was creating a monster not a garden. So many good trees were now being felled. Most of the hazel was coppiced and pollarded beyond recognition and some of the fast growers like larch barely had chance to get their roots into the ground before he felled them. It appeared to Poppy that the wood that Angus was supposed to be taking care of was being abused and to her horror visions of Mr Ivy haunted her.

Such were the demands of the garden and the villagers for free wood that a large percentage of woodland reserved for the winter months was nearly depleted in early summer. Angus had chopped so many branches from the great trees and neglected so much of his usual work of tending carefully the growth and health of the woodland that suddenly and startlingly one by one they shed their leaves. Any woodsperson knows that when plants and trees feel their survival is imperilled they will lose their leaves or fail to flower in a desperate act of survival. Angus's shock and disbelief at what he saw, instead of wakening him up to his wilful negligence, instead turned swiftly to anger and for the first time he threw his axe to the ground. What Angus did not realise was that his problems were only just beginning.

Poppy had fallen ill. She had tried to ignore it and to carry on for weeks but her small frame could only take so much pressure. The lack of good food, sleep and comfort were major factors in her deterioration, but in her usual fashion she said nothing, she did not want any fuss. Angus in his rage and single mindedness simply did not notice so Poppy carried on, at a much slower pace than normal and still clinging to the belief that sooner or later he would come to his senses.

The summer weather meant that the demand for logs was reduced. Knowing that he had kept his side of the bargain in delivering the free wood, Angus now felt he had the time to reap his reward from the villagers. Having struck a bargain with his neighbours he had not bothered them by checking that they were keeping their side of it, he just believed they would. The Fantabulous Floral was now only about a month away and it was time to visit his friends and to assess the produce.

One by one he visited the households but to his horror instead of finding a floral and vegetable spectacular he found disaster after disaster. Most of the villagers had either sowed their seeds too early and they had succumbed to the late frosts or too late producing semi mature flowers. Others had simply not bothered to sow any at all and promptly handed back their seeds. A few blamed bad weather or poor compost and any number of other trivial excuses but the awful truth was there was nothing Angus could use for his garden. Some individuals attempted to offer weak apologies, but many were just rude and uncaring.

Angus sat with his head in his hands. Had it all been for nothing?

Was he going to have to give up his dream of 'The King of Gardens'? And why had so many of the villagers let him down, did they see him as a weak man that they could treat him with such contempt? After what seemed like hours of total despair Angus finally began to think again. There was still the Fundraiser event to come and maybe people would now be shamed into ensuring that they did not let him down again and would ensure that they would be there to support him. Thinking of the Fundraiser reminded him of the previous year and an image of Mr Blackthorn sprang into his mind. Angus knew that Blackthorn was not a likable person, there was nothing gentle or kind about him, but shallow that he may be, he always got the results he wanted. Perhaps, Angus decided, he should learn some lessons from him and toughen up his approach.

At home he grew more and more flowers and vegetables; there was no time to stop and stare, no time to think about anything except his garden creation. To get the money he needed to continue growing and producing he had no choice but to increase the cost of the wood that he was supplying, no more free logs to those who had let him down so badly and no hand-outs to the needy. In addition he would charge more for his daily rate when supplying services in the community.

These changes made an immediate impact in the village. People were shocked, upset and whispers of discontent and ill feeling toward Angus were expressed. With the fundraiser event so close this was more than a little worrying, but Angus had not thought of that.

Chapter 12
The Fundraiser

Angus and Poppy had always been known to work well as a team. As a result preparing for the event was almost second nature to them. They worked tirelessly together over the next days; they put up notices on all the tree boundaries of the hamlet, they stopped travellers and asked them to spread the word on their journeys to other villages, plus they related their ideas to the local gentry. Angus was really looking forward to the fundraiser. Poppy on the other hand had her reservations. She sensed a storm brewing; she kept her thoughts to herself. She had already begun to notice that the people in the village were slowly becoming fed up with Angus's new image.

Poppy knew her husband well; she knew he wasn't a bad person and had not a bad bone in his body, but in some ways she wanted all of this to stop. If she were brutally honest with herself she wanted the fundraiser to fail. She just wanted to get back to her old life and to have her gentle and honest husband back with her.

Poppy was looking so frail, she had lost her 'zip' and spring ages ago. She no longer sang when she went into the wood and most days she forgot to take the birdseed with her. Things were truly taking their toll on poor Poppy. Angus was so wrapped up in his own mission he was failing to notice what really real matters, health and happiness. Poppy also noticed that her home and garden were beginning to look like extensions of the building site for the construction of the all-consuming garden.

The moment came for the Fundraising day. Everything that could be done was done. It was now up to the village to answer their calling.

The scene was set in the second field to the North of the village, a good sunny south facing aspect. A picturesque setting; to the left a babbling brook, to the right the woods' boundary, and in the fore ground the great majestic mountains of the middle counties. It was a glorious day without a cloud in the sky. The event was scheduled for 3p.m. allowing the villagers to do their chores or rise from their slumber. Angus started to set out the markings for the ditch jumping, put up the straw archery stands and ribboned the tug-of-war rope. The ground was firm and fresh after the last harvest of the straw and the stubble glinted in the morning sun. Poppy and some close friends put on a spread of bread, cheese, summer fruits all to be washed down with fine apple juice, all placed on a large table.

Angus waited at the gate of the field anxiously gazing down the lane for the villagers to arrive. First to arrive was Rodney Birch from the Wood Hatch pub with three casks of ale. His visit was rushed owing to the fact he had to open the pub to a waiting mob of thirsty villagers. But Angus sensed more than that. Rodney was always a polite and chatty man, but not today. It was if he was trying to say something but then just could not find the words.

Just shortly after Mr Birch's departure, Angus spotted a carriage full of people coming down the lane and his heart lifted. He started to wave his arms directing the carriage in, but the carriage stopped midway. A man emerged looking confused and disorientated and proceeded to walk to Angus. Angus asked" Are you having problems with your horses? Can I be of some assistance?" The man replied, "Oh no, it's all OK with the horses, we just seemed to have missed a turning for the market."

Angus replied, "Oh so you are not here for the fundraiser?" "Good God no, we have great business at the market!" he said.

Angus politely asked if they would consider the idea of coming in and consider having a go. The man declined the offer of joining in the sport but asked if his party could stop for a while to rest. Angus obliged and escorted the carriage in. The passengers, a large party of somewhat portly build, promptly exited the carriage. They wasted no time in spotting the food and refreshments and it seemed rude to refuse them any sustenance. With the speed of a plague of locusts, in fact the locusts might have been more forgiving, they devoured three quarters of the food on the hospitality tables. They made no attempt to ask about the event, speaking only to brag about their wealth and personal possessions. Greedy people with an appetite to suit.

Such was the mild and meek nature of their hosts that nothing was said. Angus continued to gaze down the lane, hearing what could only be described as the distant greedy laugh of their departing recent visitors.

A trickle of people slowly appeared mostly those seeking cheap drinks and none of them looking fit to participate in physical exercise. Some turned up keen to enter but their keenness did not match their ability to see the discipline through. Talk was all they had to offer along with a large appetite. A few entered the

The Fundraiser

archery competition, but teams for the tug-of-war seemed very sparse. The only busy area was the hospitality area. Angus tried to get some public spirit mobilised but his efforts were futile. No one was interested in Angus's dreams and aspirations; they were only concerned with what was in it for them.

Angus stood his ground and called out "You were willing to take my wood in the winter months, willing to eat and drink my hospitality but not willing to give anything back!"

His words served only to make what was increasingly looking like a mob angrier. Above the noise Angus heard someone shout "Most of the village is against your greedy ways Angus, parading around trying to be something that you are not!" The lack of any countering response served only as confirmation of those accusations.

At this point Poppy was at her wits end. She saw the advancing mob move towards her husband and impulsively she threw herself between the two groups. Her screams of, "Stop, stop please stop!" was enough to silence all. It was at that point she collapsed on the floor. Angus instantly raced to her aid and showed the most affection towards her than he had for many a month. The silence was deafening. Angus picked up his wife and carried her out of the field.

Hercules saw this and pulled his cart to meet his master. The devotion shown to them both was magical to see. Everyone slowly dispersed from the field leaving only the drunkest to carry on and drink the unattended barrels of beer.

Angus returned home with Poppy. He was full of shame and remorse. What he had done and the person he had become had caused this pain and illness in the person he most loved. When Poppy regained a little strength she asked only for one thing from her husband, that he returned their life to normal. Her words to him were "Let it go!"

Angus's answer was a swift, "I will."

Chapter 13

Poppy's Illness

Poppy quickly fell asleep but Angus sensed that something wasn't right. For several days following he tended her fever. She had lost a lot of weight and had little strength to recover. He was at his wits end. One evening as he gently wiped her fevered brow he remembered a story that that he heard many years ago about a herbalist who had lived in the woods close to the edge of the shire. It was quite possible that he had died some time ago but Angus knew that that this could be his only chance to save Poppy and so reluctantly he decided he must leave her alone at the house and go out to see if he could locate this man.

Outside he was surprised to find Hercules waiting for him almost as though the old horse knew what he must do. Angus mounted Hercules and together they set off on their journey. Hercules carried his master for hours through fields and woods he barely recognised but by now Angus was so exhausted that he could do nothing but put his faith in his trusty friend. Hours later they came across a very old and ramshackle house positioned on the edge of a strange green forest where the variety of evergreens was unfamiliar even to Angus. Hercules stopped and dropped his head in front of the doorstep. "Surely no one lives here?" exclaimed Angus but Hercules just shook his head as if to say "Here we are!" Angus dismounted and knocked on the door. Two men appeared at the door, both bearded and somewhat green in appearance, later explained by the fact they were covered in spinach that they had just consumed for their dinner.

"We were expecting you Angus," they said together.

"Pardon" said Angus in amazement, " You were expecting me?"

"Yes," they replied in unison, "Come on in." One of them walked Angus into the house whilst the other gave Hercules a gentle stroke and a nose bag to feed from. The two very elderly men introduced themselves as Mr Willow and Mr Yew and went on to explain that they had long known of Angus's need for greatness and admiration. "The whispers came through the trees. We heard of your greed and carelessness which left them so many people unhappy and the woodland so neglected."

"How could this be?" asked Angus and listened with astonishment to their reply."

"From the beginning of time caretakers have been bestowed the trust of the woods. This was their duty and their responsibility but none to date have been as ruthless as you. For some reason your trees have always thought you had goodness inside you and they have waited patiently for you to return to your senses but now it is reaching a critical point and their leaf drop could soon become critical. Poppy on the other hand always stood firm to her duties to the wood, by just being calm and talking sweetly to them all."

Mr Willow went on to explain that for years respect and good will toward Angus had stretched further than the village or any distant show, but recently the stories they were hearing, whispered by travellers passing through the woods were telling a very different story.

Angus sat down in total shock and then to his horror he burst into tears, something he had never done before let alone in front of strangers.

But it was only received with a gentle smile. "You must be strong for Poppy, and that is why we were called to help you, with a little help from Hercules."

Mr Willow said, "Once your wife is strong enough give her this substance called Taxodium, extracted from my yew tree it will give her strength and help her to regain some weight. It will take some time for her to recover, so you must be patient. Your time has come to give your wife some nursing and caring. My God she deserves it! Go quickly and always remember your actions in life affect not only yourself but everyone around you. Respect your woodland and try to listen to its' needs, without them we would all perish."

Angus turned and left, eventually arriving home by the first quarter of the moon. Thankfully Poppy was still resting and knew nothing of his journey to save her. He immediately gave her the aspirin and prescribed further rest. A kiss on the forehead brought a small smile.

Angus had learned a painful lesson in life. He vowed never to return to his past alter ego. He realised that that the love of his wife and the self- respect he had gained from doing a good days work looking after his woodland and caring for his neighbours were worth so much more than the transient glory of winning competitions at any cost. Poppy did regain full health and got what she wished for, her husband freed from what she thought of his temporary madness and a return to their simple but wholesome life. Angus slowly regained respect within the village and along with his neighbours they all played their part in society.

The village and all its inhabitants along with Angus, Poppy and Hercules were then lost in time until all that remained was a distant echo. The trees continued to whisper their stories in the wind to anyone who cared to listen and understand.

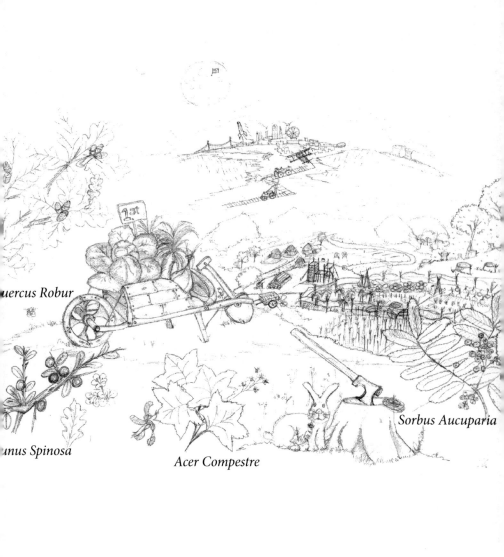

Quercus Robur

Sorbus Aucuparia

Prunus Spinosa

Acer Compestre

Part 2

Modern Times

Many years had passed, the earth was a lot older when we revisit and restart this story. Humankind's interventions in the environment had effected a dramatic change on the landscape. A far cry from the past told in the recent chapters.

People had developed huge machines to move land and sea to fit their own vision of how their world should look. They were still possessed of the same core values such as greed and selfishness running alongside generosity and kindness. The rich eco system of trees and open meadows and swamps had been torn up and discarded to meet the ever increasing demands of a growing population. Roads were created to speed up the need to go forward rapidly, carving up Ancient woodlands plus bridging massive river and channel expanses. The pace of humankind had accelerated the warmth of the land and seas to the detriment of their local environment. The trees were decimated, their need to grow limited within tight boundaries. Some still cared for them, others capitalised on them. The demand for steel and oil, plus an ever hungry world encroached massively on woodlands, forests and jungles the world over.

Chapter 14

A New Beginning

Trendlewood village had long since gone. Its replacement was a huge reservoir which served to cover up all known trace of the villagers. Angus's great wood still stood but was considerably less in size due to arable crop expansion. Angus and Poppy's house was gone, swallowed up by the land over the years of decay. The meadow still stood where the vegetables and flowers had grown. Grazing sheep chewed on the sweet grass benefitting from years of good soil growth. The wood was being sold off along with the meadows at a local auction. Planning permission would be granted if the new owners would manage the Ancient woodland. But any living abode or structure must be blended and sympathetic to the landscape of outstanding natural beauty.

New families had moved into the area. The first of these was the Dillinger family, Dad Dave, Mum Sue, and baby Jack. Dave was an acclaimed architect who had created and designed many modern buildings throughout the world. He was ethically sound in his commitment to the materials used on his buildings, something of an ecowarrior but behind a desk. His heart was truly in the right place and he had earned his place in society by hard study and positive career choices, a product of human greatness.

His wife Sue was a nurse taking timeout to raise little baby Jack. Her need to care for people at an early age made her who she is, a perfect match to her husband Dave. They were not perfect, but then no-one is but their goals and visions were the same. She had worked in some of the top hospitals in the country and loved her work but now she had resisted promotion to staff nurse to create a family of her own.

Baby Jack, well he is just baby Jack, his future is still to be written. He has been given the perfect start in life and his happy disposition even seemed to dull some of the pain of early teething, much to the relief of his parents.

They lived in the hustle and bustle of London town where they became increasingly concerned for Jack's health in the highly polluted metropolis. Most of their friends' older children had lung problems and frequent coughs and colds and although many of them blamed their environment, few could see a way to get off the conveyor belt.

Dave and Sue however craved for clean air and a slower pace of life and they began to make their plans to move to the countryside. They had seen their opportunity of a fresh start on the internet advertising the auction of the wood and meadow (Angus and Poppy's wood and meadow) aptly named Bluebell wood.

Luckily for them they had the freedom to change their location and lifestyle at the drop of a hat. Dave had always dreamed of building his own home, but the setting had to be perfect. Bluebell wood seemed to be that setting. They had seen this idyllic location on the World Wide Web, and decided to act without delay. Such was the power of technology that serious parties bidding for Bluebell wood were able to do so from their own homes. The only local interest came from farmers and one man wishing to open up a frog farm.

Bidding started slowly for Bluebell wood until a realistic price got to the table, then the race was on. The clicking of computer buttons, bleeps and blips of mobile phones all contributed to the final two horse race.

The Dillingers and an unknown property developer were left to slug it out. Dave's resolve saw him win. His need was much more personal and environmentally sound rather than his fellow bidder's concentration on the profit margin. The final hammer was sounded. Dave, Sue and Jack were the proud new owners of Bluebell wood along with four acres of land. They celebrated at home with an ice cream. "This was all meant to be!"

Luck seemed to be on the side of Family Dillinger; little did they know that their recent good fortune would be the beginning of a lengthy wrangle with the local planning department over planning permission.

David's vision of their new home called upon all his expertise, his eco credentials and his grit and determination. His plan was to blend his proposed structure into the hillside, on the site of a sunken retreat, fit it with a green roof and modern glass frontage. His final proposal swayed the planning department in his favour. He proposed using coppiced and pollarded wood from the wood to help clad and finish off at the exposed concrete areas. The planning team appreciated his idea and swiftly granted planning provided a percentage of replanting of nature trees to the North side of the wood was carried out.

Dave took little time commissioning a builder to help build his new home. Sue was in charge of fittings and fixtures; Jack was in charge of colour schemes owing to his love of hand painting on all wall surfaces at home. Money and a great mind as well as a belief to see a project through efficiently and smoothly meant that the family home was completed within a year of planning approval.

Once in, the Dillingers quickly adjusted to their new surroundings. The peaceful countryside suited them well. Gone was the madness and rush of the city. The nearest thing to rush hour was the village school run, or the blocking of the lanes by herded cattle. Dave worked from home and seldom left his office. Some days he had to go to site meetings, but always came home if the traffic was heavy. This suited Sue and Jack perfectly. Sometimes Sue missed her friends and family but she decided to join the local crèche and mums' group some miles away, if only to amuse an ever curious Jack. Dave in the meantime joined the local pub darts team and spent many a pleasant evening there. Other new ideas like a small raised bed of flowers and vegetables were introduced, all in a bit of fun. The produce was not intended to sustain their diet as Angus had previously had to do, large local supermarkets more than provided choice and abundance from all around the world, and all year through. But It was nice to see the essence of past times being resurrected. As time passed Sue's skills grew in horticulture. She was up to growing beans by the end of the year.

The one thing Sue was uncertain about was the Bluebell Wood. To her it seemed to be very uninviting. Sadly the world was more scary and untrusting than in previous times. Locked doors, security systems and a more cautious population meant that neighbours no longer ran in and out of each other's homes and new comers to a community find it more difficult to find a sense of place in villages or even to feel free to explore their surroundings. So Sue and Jack never ventured any further than the wood's perimeter.

Busy lives and work commitments saw David spending more time away from his family on bigger projects abroad. Sue realised this had to happen from time to time and accepted it. Being close to nature was always a nice thought. When Dave returned home he could just switch off and unwind. Sue and Jack took the long days as a chance to broaden their gardening skills and plant knowledge. They started to introduce pollen rich plants for bees and butterflies plus starting a small holding for chickens. The local farmer Mr Parrish, worked the existing land for hay and sometimes introduced the odd cow or sheep for little Jack's amusement.

As the family began to ease into their new life Sue became ever more intrigued about the bluebell wood. Jack was nearly 4 and he had just seen his first rabbit; it had popped out of the woodland, sniffed the air, and then popped back in. This made Jack laugh. Their wood had something more to offer than just a dark gloomy outlook. Dave also commissioned a group of tree surgeons to make safe some unsafe limbs going over the road. This was on the North side of the wood, well away from the house, but the noise made both Jack and Sue wonder what all the fuss was about. As Sue and Jack walked the perimeter they found themselves ever tempted to walk in. The day was very warm and the shade of the trees made them cool, which relaxed Sue. The tree workers had opened up a small piece of wood to take in their machinery. They found themselves walking in mud. To their delight a cool breeze picked up, riffling through the trees and creating an array of dappled light on the ground. Sue looked at Jack, he was mesmerised by the leaves as they gently lifted in the wind. This prompted Sue to sing a nursery rhyme of a rose garden, when the dappled light shone gently on the woodland flowers. Suddenly a rabbit hopped out from the undergrowth; Jack laughed and took chase. Sue frantically took chase after Jack but he was too nimble, nipping under low branches and shrubs. The panic set in in Sue's voice. Jack seemed to be heading ever closer to the tree surgeons noisy chainsaws. Jack was in her sights. He stopped suddenly and turned around, Sue had only her eyes fixed upon her son and failed to notice a protruding branch. The knockout blow was delivered just metres away from smiling Jack. Sue suffered a momentary loss of consciousness and as she recovered she had this vision of a wooden house amongst a field of flowers and vegetables and amidst the sound of the gently swaying branches of the old trees she seemed to hear a voice whispering "make it so all will be at peace". She awoke with a cool breeze over her and little Jack sitting by her smiling saying, "I saw the wooden people." Sue instantly got up and hugged him, "Did you?" she replied. Jack said "I saw the wooden house". They then stood up together and calmly hand in hand walked home as if nothing really happened.

That night Sue had the strangest dream about a family who lived in a wooden house; they had a big shire horse, they were happy with their life and lived a simple self-sufficient existence in a totally sustainable way. Sue appreciated their life and smiled in her dream, she woke very gently the next day. The lump on her head had gone down a bit, but was still a bit sore; nevertheless, she woke in a good frame of mind.

Jack ran into her bedroom holding a piece of paper on which he had done a drawing. Sue was amazed at what she saw. The picture was almost a perfect picture of Sue's vision of the wooden house. It had an arching roof of wooden tiles, two supporting tree trunks held the roof up. In the middle was a big wooden door slightly ajar to give the house a welcoming feeling. The walls of the house consisted of log uprights which curved gently nestling the beautiful flowers that flanked the doorway. A pile of chopped wood was neatly stacked near the doorway in a pyramid formation; everything was just so, nothing looked out of place. Sue smiled at Jack and asked how he came across this picture. Jack replied that he drew it after speaking to the wooden people yesterday. Sue then went on to explain that she had dreamt of the wooden people. "We need to keep this a secret until daddy gets home tomorrow." That day Jack continued to draw quite freely the garden picture on anything he could lay his hands on. Sue was deeply pre-occupied with housework, smiling and joking with little Jack in between chores. For the first time Sue was at total ease with her home, she appreciated the small things in life as a great gift. Things like a warm sunny day, the clean air and the mix of wild flowers in the meadow.

Since Jack had discovered his new found skill he had managed to create some admiring attention from other mums and children in the crèche and mum's group. It wasn't long before someone suggested that they should enter a local gardening show held annually in May in the 3 shires showground and base their entry on Jack's drawings. Sue was increasingly becoming a good gardener with her home grown pickles and jams making quite a mark within the mum's group. She warmed to the idea but saw a hurdle as to who would build this garden. One lady said "Well Dave is an architect, he must know some builders." That evening, sitting around the family table, Sue put the question to Dave. Jack had been allowed to stay up late to add his enthusiasm and to join in the vote. Dave was not a selfish man and wanted the best for his son. The idea was plausible on paper, but who would project manage it? At that point Sue and Jack pulled out and put on two bright yellow hard hats and looked at each other. Dave saw the funny side and agreed immediately to draw up the plans to make the garden structurally sound.

So the dream team Dillinger began. Money was no object and like all of Dave's projects the idea swiftly moved from concept to the real thing. Sue contacted the local nursery to source and supply the plants, seeds and vegetables; Jack provided the pictures and Dave supplied the work force and space to build.

They also decided that after the show the garden would be donated to a local children's hospice for all to see. Jack also had become a bit of a local celebrity for his design, even attracting some media attention and thoughts of a book on the horizon. The family would see how things would pan out and never expected too much from this. Dave was a trustee for a regional woodland charity and saw this as a great opportunity to embrace the issues that had troubled him for some time. To help raise awareness of the plight of the ever

71

decreasing woodland areas, he now found himself in a position to begin to influence local government and land owners. All of this from a single encounter in Bluebell Wood.

Money can buy a lot of things in life but can never guarantee happiness. David and his family were level headed; they appreciated what they had but also understood the need to work hard it. The garden united them in a way that they had never dreamt of. By giving something back to the land they felt that in their own small way they were making the world into a better place.

The Three Shires show was a couple of weeks away. The Dillingers were quite relaxed with their approach to the build-up. For them it was all a bit of fun, any idea of winning was quickly dismissed and laughed off. The gardens exhibited at the show ranged from a beach garden all the way to an oasis. The quality was always high. Many designers saw this as a platform for bigger and better things in their career, but the Dillingers were just happy to be there.

The garden was ready to be installed. The build time was two weeks but David was meticulous in his execution to the build. The articulated lorry turned up four days before the opening, on site, with what could only be described as a flat pack garden. Sue and Jack looked on in their yellow hats from their campervan with great excitement. Every section was numbered and was fork lifted into place. By the end of the day the garden was finished ready to plant. The fellow exhibitors just stood and watched in awe. The Dillingers were reservedly happy they were not show offs.

The next stage was planting which was as equally impressive. A separate articulated lorry was needed.

Sue was completely taken aback by the size of the garden plus the amount of plants supplied by the nursery. The pressure started to build on her. Dave was in the wings if she wanted help, but didn't want to make matters worse. Sue was a beginner in horticulture, Dave had no idea and Jack... well he just smiled and played with his new found toy, Mr Wheelbarrow. The nearby wood provided silence for thinking and seemed the natural place to retreat to. Dave was left playing with Jack giving Sue some valuable time out. Up to this point Sue had only supplied guidance and support to the garden project. She didn't want to let her family down, but the family had faith in her judgement, yet inside she felt uneasy.

She walked deeper into the wood and saw a nice sunny clearing in the middle. A strange sensation came over her. A group of very old Yews encircled what could only be a large prehistory grain pit in which the remains of a chimney stack was visible. She was drawn to the centre and promptly sat down on an old tree stump. A split second was all that was needed to transfer Sue back in time to a world long forgotten. The house was the very same home of Mr Yew and Mr Willow, the mysterious wood dwellers who had come to Angus's aid. A visitor appeared who was strangely familiar. Sue could see his anguish. Then another revelation unfolded to a very familiar household situated in a wood surrounded by a vegetable field and beautiful gardens.

A shire horse stood outside waiting at the door. A very large man appeared, hurriedly mounted the horse and rode off. Sue felt compelled to enter this familiar house. Someone was in pain. Her nursing instincts kicked in. A very petite frail lady lay on a bed made of straw. Her image was not fitting to her age. Sue had seen this on the oncology wards at the hospital. She was surrounded by beautiful flowers. Such colours were a dazzling sight to see. How lucky she was to have such a caring husband. Suddenly, Sue's head cleared and she realised that the vision she had just had of the wood and the home and garden from had given her an answer to her current problem.

She hurried back to the garden and went to work filling out the planted area. She had to do it swiftly so as not to lose the inspiration of her recent dream. Dave and Jack could only watch and admire her speed of progress. By the end of the third day her work was finished a day early, prior to judging. This did not concern them. They had fulfilled a dream inspired by the trees and a past life, a far cry from Modern times.

All other fellow exhibitors had also completed their gardens a day early, which gave the Dillinger family time to meet and greet their fellow competitors. The mood was softened by smiling Jack's appearance. He was dressed in dungarees and wellingtons with a big straw hat on his head. Many of the exhibitors were tense and nervous after months of preparation but the Dillingers were calm and happy, pleased only to have realised their garden dream.

Judging was done in secret, a winner was confirmed and every one returned the following day to learn of their fate. Medals of bronze, silver and gold were awarded to a mixture of gardens. Some competitors received their awards in good humour others in disappointment but in the main the feeling was of good sportsmanship.

As for the Dillingers, they received a gold best in show award much to the great joy from fellow exhibitors and public alike. Sue, Jack and Dave were totally surprised to win but kept calm not wishing to show off. Press and media soon turned up to congratulate them. The family left little Jack to do the interviews and TV appearances. The woodland charity got press, their plight for all to see, with many landowners signing up for woodland restoration within the three shires.

Sue felt pleased for the family's win but knew she could not take all the credit. A secret party was involved in the creation of this wonderful garden. She wished that they could be here to share the glory but in reality it will never happen or will it?

Towards the end of the show the family were taking a well-deserved back seat from the public's constant admiration. Jack was first to notice some movement in the nearby wood. His reaction was to say the words "The wooden people are here." Sue and Dave turned to look. On the forest edge were four figures almost camouflaged by their surroundings. Sue looked at Jack and started to cry. "Yes Jack it's the wooden people." Dave, a little confused asked, "Do you know them?"

Sue replied, "Only in my dreams. They are the reason we are here." The wind then picked up gently and they were gone. Jack said "Bye, bye wooden people." The wooden people would never show themselves again but lived within the Dillingers' hearts. They respected their wood and encouraged others to do the same. After all without them we won't be here.

The End

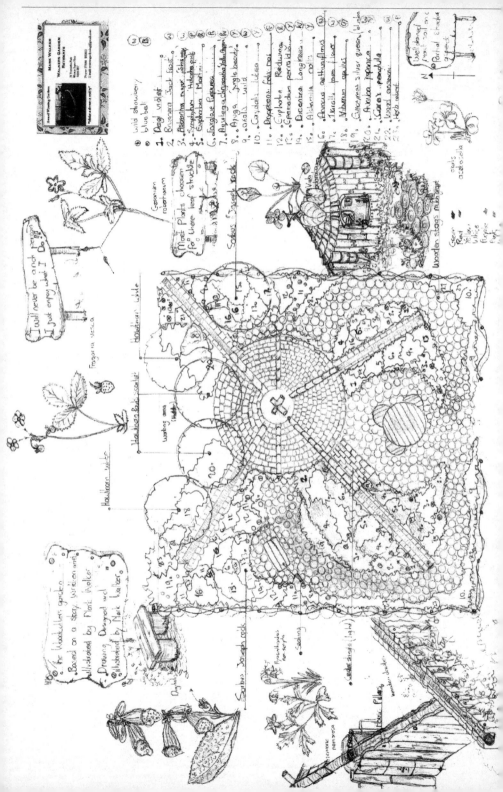

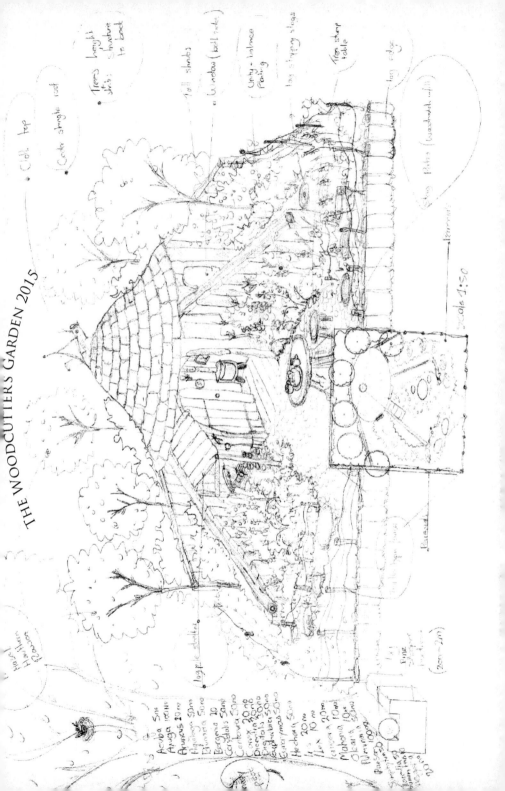

THE WOODCUTTERS GARDEN 2015